Text copyright © Brian Morse 1997
Illustrations copyright © David Browne 2001

First published in 1997
by Macdonald Young Books

This edition published in 2009 by Wayland

A catalogue record for this book is available from
the British Library.

ISBN: 978 0 7502 5747 3

Printed in China

Wayland
338 Euston Road, London NW1 3BH

Wayland is a division of Hachette Children's Books,
an Hachette UK Company
www.hachette.co.uk

Plant Attack

BRIAN MORSE

Illustrated by David Browne

WAYLAND

Chapter One

Adam arrived home from school at four o'clock. Outside was a bitterly cold February day – the air smelt of snow – but inside was warm. He dropped his coat and bag on the floor and shouted, "Mum, tea ready?" Then he noticed the plant.

The plant stood on the table next to the radiator. It had glossy green leaves and was covered with tendrils like miniature creepers.

"Mum!" Adam called.

Mum didn't answer but there were voices in the kitchen: hers, Dad's and someone else's.

Adam walked closer to the kitchen door. He peered at the plant. He wasn't quite sure he liked the look of it. It looked as if... well, it might sound stupid, but *as if it were hungry*.

"She said it was the best plant-hunting expedition she'd ever been on," a woman's voice said. "Brilliant."

Dad asked a question.

"The Amazon," she said. "You can't keep Ms Grandison away from there!"

Plant hunting! Adam thought. Sounds really dangerous! Fancy being attacked by a wild daisy!

Something was tickling his neck. He tried to brush it off but the second he took his fingers away the feeling returned.

He scrunched up his neck. That made no difference.

"Must go," the woman said. "The plant I've left to deliver must be feeling really miserable."

"Miserable!" Dad laughed.

"Plants from the Amazon hate cold," the woman said.

Adam's neck was itching again. The feeling went right across the back of his neck. It touched his throat.

He stepped back and turned. The plant swayed slightly. Half a dozen tendrils twitched in the draught.

Adam laughed. "Trying to strangle me, were you?" he said.

The kitchen door opened and a woman stood there. "Talking to your new plant, are you?" she smiled. "It will love that!"

Mum said, "Adam, this lady's from the Rare Plant Society. She's brought a plant for Dad to look after  for them." Mum and Dad had a garden centre. Dad's speciality was indoor plants. "They want to know how well it will do in this country."

The woman winked at the plant. "Be good!" she said. "And keep wrapped up warm! Bye, Adam!"

Chapter Two

Later that evening Adam looked out of the
kitchen window. A blizzard was blowing.
The garden was several centimetres deep
in snow.

"Mum!" he called excitedly. "Come and
see!"

Mum looked worried.

"Your brother—" she said. "He's very
late."

"Yes, where's he gone?" Adam asked. Gary was in Year Eight at secondary school.

"His class went on a trip. They should be home by now," Mum said. "Perhaps the motorway's blocked." She went into the front room where Dad was watching a nature programme on television.

Suddenly Adam noticed Babs, their tortoiseshell cat. Babs was crouched, staring at the hall door. The fur on the back of her neck was standing on end. She was growling too, deep in her throat, the way she did at the dog next door.

"What's up? Has something frightened you?" Adam said. He pushed the door wide open. Babs spat. She flattened herself against the floor. You could hardly see anything of her except her eyes.

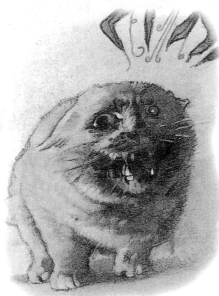

"It's only Dad's new plant," Adam said, puzzled. "Nothing to be scared of."

Except the plant was on the other end of the table. Nothing strange about that, of course. Someone might have moved it. But Adam got the impression the plant had just stopped moving itself, that if he'd gone straight through the door he'd have caught it in the act.  He remembered the creepy sensation he'd had earlier when he'd been standing next to it.

Before he had time to think about that the front door crashed open. A snowman stumbled in.

"Ace weather!" Gary said. "Brill!"

"The door, Gary!" Dad called. "Be careful, we've had a particularly delicate plant delivered!"

Before Gary could get the door shut Babs darted down the hall. She shot between Gary's legs and leaped out into the blizzard.

"Wow!" he said. "What's up with Babs? You usually have to throw her outside in weather like this."

Dad had his hands on the hall radiator. "I hate to tell you but I think the central heating's broken down," he said. "I thought it was getting cold. The only place we're going to keep warm tonight is in bed."

Then he looked at the plant. "Oh, no!" he said. "How are we going to keep that warm? It's travelled thousands of miles to get here. We can't let it come to any harm."

"That's easy," Mum said. "We'll put all the electric heaters in Gary's bedroom, get the boys to share one bed and the plant can keep warm in there too."

Chapter Three

Later Adam fell asleep alone in the
unfamiliar room.

When he woke Gary still hadn't come to
bed.

The heat was tropical. Adam pushed the
cover off.

Something moved in the darkness.

"Babs?" Adam said drowsily. "Came
back, did you?" He put a hand out.

A damp nose touched his fingers. Something cold and smooth licked then tugged at his thumb.

"Not biting me, are you?" Adam laughed. His thumb was tugged again.

There was a quick swishing, slithering sound.

Not Babs!

With a yelp of fear Adam sat up trembling. As he put the bedside lamp on there was a violent rustling in the darkness.

A handful of the plant's tendrils hung down from the table. It was those he'd touched. Yuck!

Or had the plant touched him?

Adam edged away across the bed to a safe distance.

Very slowly he sank back down and pulled the bedclothes back up. What a good job he hadn't called out! He could just imagine what Gary would have said!

"Mum – you know that plant? It's sitting up reading! It won't let Adam put the light out!"

He left the light on though. The plant – there was something not quite right about it.

Suddenly he noticed some of its tendrils grasping the table lamp. Adam knew from Dad that plants can often do extraordinary things most people just wouldn't believe. But it had only been in the room a little time. Wasn't that too fast for a plant to move?

Then he must have fallen asleep again. He found himself waking with a bang.

The plant wasn't in the middle of the table any more. Its creepers weren't wrapped round the lamp. Half were waving about in the air close to his head, the other half clamped on to the edge of the table.

It had been about to leap down on him!

Chapter Four

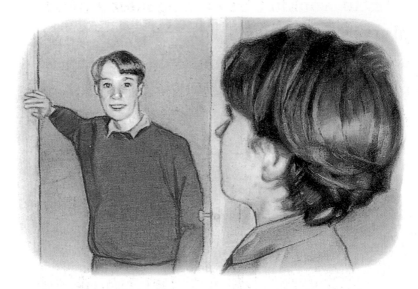

As Adam jumped out of bed the door flew open.

"Mucking about?" Gary said. "I thought you would be. You haven't messed with my things have you?" He looked around suspiciously.

"The plant!" Adam said.

"Ugly, isn't it?" Gary began undressing. "Do you know Ms Grandison, the woman who found it, discovered nearly two hundred new plants in the Amazon?"

Adam pointed. "It's alive."

"Dad wouldn't be looking after a dead plant for them, would he?" Gary said. He came round Adam's side of the bed and picked it up.

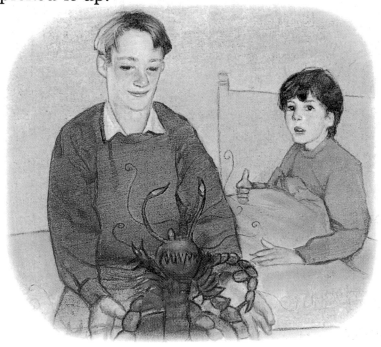

"Don't!" Adam said in alarm.

"What do you think it's going to do?" Gary said. "Bite?" He replaced it. "One plant Ms Grandison discovered she called the Devil Plant."

"Why?" Adam said.

"Waahh!" Gary said. His hands snaked in Adam's direction.

Adam nearly jumped out of his skin.

"Haven't you ever seen that old film about plants taking over the world?" Gary asked.

"What happens in it?"

"Everyone goes blind and there are these plants called Triffids that roam around spitting poison at people." Gary shuddered. "Ace! Brill!" He jumped into bed.

"Why was it called the Devil Plant?" Adam insisted.

"It ate people, I expect," Gary said.

"Gary!"

"Just kidding!"

"Gary, let me sleep that side, please!" Adam pleaded.

"Oh, anything for a quiet life!" Gary rolled over. Adam gratefully ran round and clambered in.

When Gary had switched the light off the snow outside made the room bright. You could still see the plant.

"Keep still!" Gary grumbled.

"Couldn't we put the plant on the landing?" Adam said. The only answer was a snore.

Adam kept watch in the moonlight, but tiredness quickly defeated him. He fell asleep himself.

Chapter Five

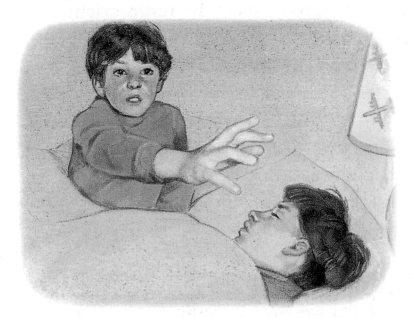

How much later it was Adam had no idea but he woke with a jolt.

The plant! He rolled over and looked.

It had gone from the table!

He shook Gary.

"What's the matter?" Gary said sleepily.

"The plant's gone! I'm putting the light on!"

"Don't you dare!" came Gary's voice.

"It could be anywhere!"

"What's it done?" Gary said. "Eaten your socks?"

Gary could make as much fun of him as he wanted. Adam leant over and put on the bedside lamp.

Gary sat up, furious. "All right! Where've you hidden it? I'm counting, Adam – five, four…"

Adam gave a frightened shout. He dived off the end of the bed.

"What's up now?"

"Look!"

"Where?"

"Above you – hanging from the light switch!"

Gary looked up. The plant was above him, clinging to the cord.

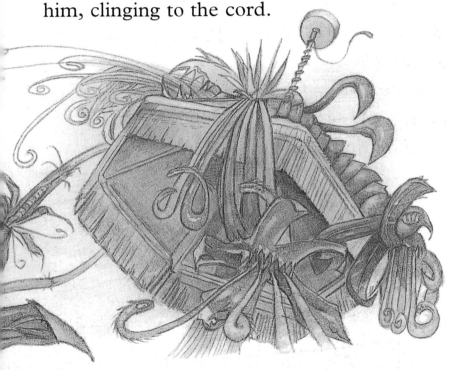

"Very clever," Gary said. "What did you use? Glue? Sticky tape? Why's this plant got you so excited? I'm warning you that if..."

Gary fell silent. Gently he slipped out from under the covers and carefully crawled down the bed to join his brother.

"It moved!" he said quietly. "I saw it too!"

A dozen tendrils suddenly shot out. They grasped the mobile of a plane hanging from the ceiling. The plant swung from the light cord to the mobile. It hung between the boys and the door.

"It's nearly twice as big as when I came to bed," Gary said.

"We're trapped! HELP!" Adam shouted at the top of his voice. "MUM! DAD!"

"Mum and Dad went out," Gary said quietly.

"In this weather? Where?"

"Down the garden centre. They wanted to borrow the big heater from the office for their bedroom."

"And left us with this?" Adam said. "They can't have!"

Chapter Six

A quarter of an hour passed. The plant grew. And grew. And grew. Its branches thickened. The leaves swelled. The tendrils grew longer.

"Why aren't they back?" Adam demanded.

Gary said nothing. He just looked petrified.

Suddenly the aeroplane mobile wobbled under the plant's weight.

"This is stupid. I'm getting out!"

But Adam didn't get anywhere. The plant shifted as if it couldn't wait to pounce on him.

Dad sold a plant called a Venus Fly Trap at the garden centre. That ate insects. But this plant was a hundred times bigger and still growing. What did *it* eat?

A bunch of tendrils as thick as an arm shot out and grasped the lampshade above the boys' heads. As the plant swung across the boys tumbled into the only space left, between the wardrobe and the window.

The tendrils stretched in the boys' direction. They didn't quite reach but they would soon.

A sweet sickly smell filled the room.

"Look," Gary said. "It's grown a flower."

The flower was crimson red, tinged with yellow.

"If Mum and Dad don't get back soon," Adam said, "we're finished."

"Watch out!" Gary shouted.

The plant had made a grab for Adam's hair.

The tendrils snaked in his direction again. They seized his arm.

"Gary! Help!" Adam cried. "It's really strong!"

Together, slowly, they prised the tendrils off. They'd torn the arm of Adam's pyjamas.

Out of reach, but only just, they cowered by the window.

"It's all sticky!" Gary said in disgust. He tried to rub the stuff off his hands. "At this rate it will fill the whole room."

"Listen! What's that?" Adam said fearfully.

Something was at the window clawing to get in. He hadn't thought the nightmare could get worse.

Chapter Seven

Whatever was outside scratched and scratched at the glass.

The plant stopped swaying. It seemed to listen too.

"Right! I'm looking!" Gary said at last. He stood up and pulled back the curtains. "It's Babs!"

The cat was on the window-sill.

"Don't let her come in!" Adam said anxiously.

"Look!" Gary said, staring back into the room. There was horror in his voice.

"There are more plants. It's multiplying!"

Out of the corner of his eye Adam saw a dozen miniature plants. He also saw the way the flower was opening like a mouth. But he was thinking of something else, remembering how Dad had worried about the plant earlier.

Then he knew what to do!

"Quick! The heaters!" he shouted. "Unplug them!"

"Why?"

"It doesn't matter why! Just pull them out!" Adam shouted. "You're the nearest! NOW! Before it stops you! Gary – DO IT!"

Adam undid the window catch. He heaved the window up. Babs miaowed, her eyes wide with terror. She didn't try to come in.

A flurry of snow and a gust of arctic air swept into the room. The temperature fell like a stone.

"Got you!" Adam said triumphantly.

But it wasn't over yet. Far from it.

The plant flew into a frenzy. It lashed out. Its tendrils pulled at their hair and arms. It tried to fasten on to their legs. As the air grew colder the smaller plants scurried along the main branches as if to encourage it.

"Adam!" Gary screamed. The plant had him round his legs and neck. It began dragging him towards the flower.

Adam grasped his brother but the plant was stronger than them both together. The smaller plants swung over Adam's head.

"Get help!" Gary gasped. "Forget me!"

But the plant had hold of Adam now.
A tendril wrapped itself round his neck.
Its grip tightened. It was more and more
difficult for him to breathe. Beside him
Gary was fighting for his life.

Adam began to lose consciousness. The
fight went out of him...

Then suddenly his head hit the floor. The plant had dropped him. For a moment all he noticed was that it was colder than he would have thought possible, sub-arctic. Out of the corner of his eye he noticed Babs had crept inside the room. Babs hissed at the plant.

If Babs felt safe inside, that must mean the plant was finally dead.

Adam's eyes began to close.

Chapter Eight

The next thing Adam knew Gary was pulling him to his feet. "Let's get out of here," he said.

Gary held Babs in his arms and guided Adam. Adam stumbled across the landing.

"All that extra heat," Gary said. "That's what made it grow so fast."

As they reached the bottom of the stairs the phone rang. Adam found the strength to run. "Dad!" he shouted, but a posh woman said, "The owner of Roseacre Garden Centre, please."

"Oh, Dad's out," Adam said, breathlessly. "Can I give him a message?"

"I suppose you'd better. It *is* rather urgent. This is Ms Grandison of the Rare Plant Society. We delivered a plant to your father this afternoon," the voice went. "Well, a mistake was made. The plant he actually has is a Devil Plant. It could be dangerous. *Very dangerous.* You will let him know, won't you?"

You bet I will! Adam thought. *And now I know why it's called a Devil Plant.*

DARE TO BE SCARED!

Are you brave enough to try more titles in the Tremors series? They're guaranteed to chill your spine...

Play... if you dare by Ruth Symes

Josie can hardly believe her luck when she finds the computer game at a car boot sale. "Play... if you dare," the game challenges. So she does. Further and further she plays, each level of the game scarier than the last. Then she reaches the last level. "Play... if you dare," repeats the game. But if she does, she could be trapped for ever...

The Claygate Hound by Jan Dean

On the school camp to Claygate, Billy is determined to scare everyone with his terrifying stories of the Claygate Hound, a vicious ghost dog said to lurk nearby. Ryan and Zeb ignore his warnings and explore the woods. They hear a ghostly howl – and run. Has Billy been speaking the truth, or is there a more terrifying reason for what they have heard?

The Curse of the Frozen Loch by Anthony Masters

Why does the ghostly figure skate the loch in the dead of night? And what is wrong with Great-Aunt Fiona? Will and Sarah are determined to solve the mystery and save Fiona. But will they be the next victims of the curse of the frozen loch?

The Ghosts of Golfhawk School by Tessa Potter

Martin and Dan love frightening the younger children at school with scary ghost stories. But then Kirsty arrives. Kirsty claims that she can actually see ghosts. Then a mysterious virus sweeps through the school. Martin is still sure she is lying. After all – ghosts don't exist, do they?

All these books and many more can be purchased from your local bookseller. For more information about Tremors, write to: The Sales Department, Hachette Children's Books, 338 Euston Road, London NW1 3BH.